# The GIANT ANIMALS Series™

# Hippos

Marianne Johnston

The Rosen Publishing Group's
PowerKids Press™
New York

Published in 1997 by The Rosen Publishing Group, Inc.
29 East 21st Street, New York, NY 10010

First Edition

Book Design: Kim Sonsky

Photo Credits: Front and back cover and p. 8 © Mark Newman/International Stock; pp. 4, 14, 17, 18, 21© Ronn Maratea/International Stock; p. 6 © M & C Denis HUOT/GLMR/Gamma Liason; p. 7 © Wildlife Conservation Society headquartered @ The New York Zoological Society; p. 11 © Jonathan Mills/International Stock; p. 12 © Henry Mills/International Stock.

Johnston, Marianne.
    Hippos / Marianne Johnston.
        p.      cm. — (The giant animals series)
    Includes index.
    Summary: Examines the physical characteristics, habits, and natural environment of the hippopotamus.
    ISBN 0-8239-5145-6 (lib. bdg.)
    1. Hippopotamus—Juvenile literature. [1. Hippopotamus.] I. Title. II. Series. Johnston, Marianne. Giant animals series.
    QL737.U57J64  1996
    599.63'5—dc21                          96-37464
                                             CIP
                                                    AC

Manufactured in the United States of America

# CONTENTS

# WHAT IS A HIPPOPOTAMUS?

Hippopotamuses, or hippos, are huge animals that spend most of their time in the water. They are **mammals** (MAM-elz). They can stay underwater for up to five minutes. In deep water, a hippo can sink to the bottom of a lake or river, where it can take an underwater walk.

Hippos are peaceful animals that have no enemies except humans who hunt them.

The hippopotamus gets its strange name from the Greek language. Its name means "river horse."

◀ A hippo likes to swim and sit in the water.

5

# TWO KINDS OF HIPPOS

Many years ago, there were several different kinds of hippos. Today there are only two kinds, the hippo and the **Pigmy hippo** (PIG-mee HIP-poh). Both kinds live in Africa.

Pigmy hippos live in the forests of West Africa. ▶

Pigmy hippos are much smaller than hippos and weigh about 400 pounds. They have longer legs and necks and don't spend as much time in the water as hippos. Pigmy hippos live to be about 35 years old. Hippos live to be about 45 years old.

◀ Hippos usually live longer than Pigmy hippos.

7

# WHERE DO HIPPOS LIVE?

Hippos live on the **savannas** (suh-VAN-uhz) of Africa. Most hippos live in central, eastern, and southern Africa. They usually live in groups in and around rivers and lakes. One of their favorite places is the Rift Valley, where Lake Edward and Lake George are. These are two of Africa's largest lakes.

Pigmy hippos live in West Africa in the countries of Liberia, the Ivory Coast, and Sierra Leone. They live in the forests.

◀ Because they spend so much time in the water, hippos live around lakes and rivers.

# HIPPOS ARE HUGE

The body of a hippo looks like a barrel. It is long and wide. A hippo's skin is grayish or brown. The bottom part of its body is pinkish. Hippos have thick, short legs with big, round feet. Each foot has four toes. Hippos also have short tails.

Hippos are about five feet tall and about eleven feet long. A full-grown hippo weighs about 5,000 pounds. The biggest hippos weigh as much as 7,000 pounds.

A hippo's body is shaped ▶
like a round barrel.

10

# SPECIAL SKIN

Hippos don't have any hair on their bodies. Instead, they have special skin that has a very thin layer on the outside. Water can pass through their skin pretty easily. This means that hippos lose water from their bodies a lot faster than people do. If they spend too much time in the dry air, they become **dehydrated** (dee-HY-dray-ted). This means they don't have enough water in their bodies. That's why hippos spend most of their time in the water.

◀ Although a hippo's skin is very thick, it can easily dry out.

13

A hippo's teeth, or tusks, are made of ivory.

# THE HIPPO'S HEAD

The head of a hippo is very large. The hippo has the biggest mouth of any animal except a whale. A hippo's mouth is almost two feet wide.

A hippo's head is perfect for an animal that spends a lot of time in the water. The eyes, ears, and nostrils are on the top of its head. That way, a hippo can have its whole body and most of its head underwater and still be able to see, hear, and breathe.

15

# WHAT DO HIPPOS EAT?

Hippos are **herbivores** (HER-bih-vohrz). This means they only eat plants. Hippos use their broad lips to pluck grass, leaves, and plants that grow in the water.

Hippos eat about 88 pounds of food a day. That may sound like a lot to us, but hippos weigh much more than we do. For their size, they actually take in less food than humans do. Hippos don't use much energy because they spend most of their time resting or slowly moving in the water.

The hippo's wide mouth makes it easy to eat a lot of food at once. ▶

# FEEDING TIME

At night, hippos leave the water to feed, or eat. Mothers and their babies feed together. Grown-up hippos without children **graze** (GRAYZ) by themselves.

Hippos follow paths made by other hippos. Some of these paths have been used so often that they look like roads. The paths are several miles long and lead to large grazing areas.

The hippos finish eating early in the morning. Then they go back along the paths toward the water.

◄ Mother hippos always eat with their babies.

19

# YOUNG HIPPOS

Baby hippos can swim and walk the moment they are born. They are usually born on land or in shallow water. Baby hippos weigh about 90 pounds.

The mother hippo is very **protective** (proh-TEK-tiv) of her baby. Young hippos need to stay close to their mothers. Lions, leopards, and crocodiles can't kill a grown-up hippo, but they like to hunt baby hippos and young hippos.

Young hippos like to play hide-and-seek. And they love it when their mothers give them piggyback rides!

Baby hippos stay close to their mothers after they are born. ▶

# HIPPOS AND HUMANS

Hippos have no enemies except humans. In Africa, some people hunt hippos. They use hippo meat for food and sell the hippo's **hides** (HYDZ) and ivory teeth, or tusks.

But not all humans are enemies of hippos. Many people in Africa work hard to protect the hippos by setting up national parks and preserves in which the hippos can live. Scientists study hippos in the national parks in Africa. And you can go to almost any zoo and see a hippo!

# GLOSSARY

**dehydrate** (dee-HY-drayt)  When the body does not have enough water.

**graze** (GRAYZ)  To eat grass and plants on the ground.

**hide** (HYD)  Animal skin.

**herbivore** (HER-bih-vohr)  An animal that eats only plants.

**mammal** (MAM-el)  An animal that is warm-blooded, breathes oxygen, and gives birth to live young.

**Pigmy hippo** (PIG-mee HIP-poh)  A type of smaller hippo.

**protective** (proh-TEK-tiv)  Keeping something from harm.

**savanna** (suh-VAN-uh)  Large area of grassy land.

# INDEX